PERRY at a Parrot Party

By Amanda Vinson

Tellwell Talent
www.tellwell.ca

ISBN
978-0-2288-3864-7 (Hardcover)
978-0-2288-3863-0 (Paperback)

For my son Logan, who stole my heart and gave me everything I never knew I was missing.

Perry at a Parrot party

Having fun and laughing hardy

Had a picnic on the lawn...

**Turned around and
friends were GONE!**

I must go find my friends so bright
Their red wings lighting up the night

So beautiful when they take flight
I should have kept them in my sight!

So Perry headed down the lane
To find his Parrot friends again

Zaney Zebra with your stripes
Eating grass of different types

Have you seen my friends in red?
"I have not" the Zebra said

Peter Penguin in the cold
With your cape and crown so gold

Have you seen my friends in red?
"I have not" the Penguin said

Spotty Scotty in the sun
Chasing sticks and having fun

Have you seen my friends in red?
"I have not" the Puppy said

Percy Panda, heart so true
Filling up on fresh bamboo

Have you seen my friends in red?
"I have not" the Panda said

Ozzy Orca in the ocean
Swimming with the water's motion

Have you seen my friends in red?
"I have not" the Orca said

Mr. Moon that shines so bright
Lighting up the dark black night

Shining here and other places
Moving through your different phases

Have you seen my friends in red?
"I have not" the wise Moon said

Betty Bear with cubs in tow
Walks along the Arctic snow

Have you seen my friends in red?
"I have not" the big Bear said

Benji Boots the kitty cat
Laying on his kitty mat

Have you seen my friends in red?
"I have not" the Kitty said

Looking but not finding yet
Perry Parrot starts to fret

I need to find my Parrot friends
This can't be how my story ends!

Perry thinks then has a thought
I'll head back to my picnic spot!

He went back to the picnic lawn
Where earlier his friends had gone

As he grew closer, colors shone
And what did he return upon?

His friends in red, looking so fantastic
Singing around the picnic basket!

Perry went to join the song
With eight new friends who came along!